Where Do Bears Sleep?

by Barbara Shook Hazen • pictures by Mary Morgan Van Royen

HarperFestival®
A Division of HarperCollinsPublishers

Where do bears sleep?
In a den.

Where do pigs sleep?
In a pen.

Sheep sleep in a fold
when it is cold.

They sleep in the field
when it is hot.

Chickens and turkeys rest in a roost.
They like a high, dry spot.

Horses sleep in stalls in stables.

Hoot owls rest on rooftop gables.

Cats curl in corners, huddle by doors,
sleep in heaps on sun-streaked floors
and on the tops of radiators.

Dogs sniff and stretch and
paw the ground, then yawn
and s l o w l y turn around
before they finally settle down.

They sleep on mats and cushioned chairs,
beside their masters—anywhere.

Badgers make their beds in burrows.

Field mice sleep
in warm earth furrows.

Birds rest in nests.
Some nest in a tree.
Some nest in cliffs overlooking the sea.

Some in sedges, some in hedges,
and some on ledges precariously.

But lucky you! You lay your head
on a pillow soft, on a cozy bed
with covers to warm you
and tuck you in tight,
your prayers all said,
and a small night-light,
and Teddy beside you
to keep you from fright,
and someone who loves you
to kiss you good night.

Good night. Good night.
Shhhhhhhhhh.
Sleep tight.